ready, stead

Dreamboat Zing

Philip Ridley
Illustrated by Chris Riddell

Puffin Books

PUFFIN BOOKS

Published by the Penguin Group
Penguin Books Ltd, 27 Wrights Lane, London W8 5TZ, England
Penguin Books USA Inc., 375 Hudson Street, New York, New York 10014, USA
Penguin Books Australia Ltd, Ringwood, Victoria, Australia
Penguin Books Canada Ltd, 10 Alcorn Avenue, Toronto, Ontario, Canada M4V 3B2
Penguin Books (NZ) Ltd, 182–190 Wairau Road, Auckland 10, New Zealand

Penguin Books Ltd, Registered Offices: Harmondsworth, Middlesex, England

First published 1996
10 9 8 7 6

Text copyright © Philip Ridley, 1996
Illustrations copyright © Chris Riddell, 1996
All rights reserved

The moral right of the author and illustrator has been asserted

Filmset in Monotype Bembo Schoolbook

Made and printed in England by Clays Ltd, St Ives plc

Except in the United States of America, this book is sold subject to the condition that it
shall not, by way of trade or otherwise, be lent, re-sold, hired out, or otherwise circulated
without the publisher's prior consent in any form of binding or cover other than that in
which it is published and without a similar condition including this condition being
imposed on the subsequent purchaser

"I'm so cool," said Dreamboat
Zing. "Nothing scares me."

"Don't boast," said his mother,
Mrs Zing. "And stop admiring
yourself in the mirror."

"But I'm so good-looking," said Dreamboat Zing.

"My eyes are so clear.

"My hair is so neat.

"My shirt is so clean.

"And the golden chain around my neck which says 'COOL' is particularly cool."

Then Dreamboat Zing went, "Hic!"

"Hiccups!" exclaimed Mrs Zing. "Goodness, they *do* make you look funny. Every time you go 'hic', you shake all over like a wibbly-wobbly jelly."

"Make the hiccups go!"
demanded Dreamboat Zing. "I
can't look funny! I'm cool!"

"There's only one cure for hiccups that I know of," said Mrs Zing. "Something will have to scare you."

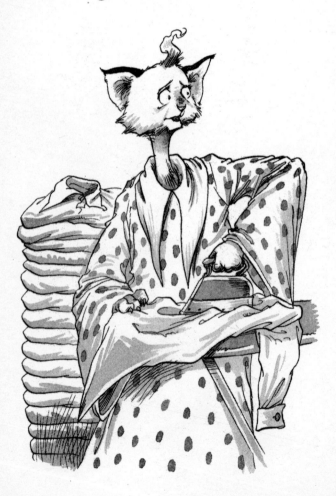

"But nothing can scare me!"
said Dreamboat Zing. "I'm too
cool!" Then added, "Hic!"

So Mrs Zing rowed Dreamboat
Zing to the middle of an ocean
and started throwing cheese and
pickle sandwiches into the water.

"What are you doing?" asked
Dreamboat Zing. Then added,
"Hic!"

"The Great White shark adores cheese and pickle sandwiches," explained Mrs Zing. "When you see a shark's mouth full of a million sharp teeth, you'll be so scared, you'll go, 'Eeek!' and your hiccups will disappear."

Suddenly, the boat rocked from side to side and a Great White shark bit Dreamboat Zing's gold necklace from his neck.

"Eeek!" went Mrs Zing.

But Dreamboat Zing merely
reached out and pulled a tooth
from the shark's jaws.

"I've made a new necklace with this tooth," he said. "Nothing scares me!"

So Mrs Zing took
Dreamboat Zing to a big,
dark cave and started to
blow up a balloon.

"What are you doing?" asked
Dreamboat Zing. Then added,
"Hic!"

"This cave is full of hungry vampire bats," explained Mrs Zing. "I'm going to burst the balloon to wake them up. When you see their flapping wings, you'll be so scared, you'll go, 'Eeek!' and your hiccups will disappear."

"BANG!" went the balloon.

Suddenly the cave was full of
vampire bats.

"Eeek!" went Mrs Zing.

But Dreamboat Zing just giggled. "The bats are tickling me," he said.

"And their wings are making
my shirt dirty – that's all! You see?
Nothing scares me!"

So Mrs Zing took Dreamboat
Zing to a volcano and dressed
them both in strange silver suits.

"What are you doing?" asked
Dreamboat Zing. Then added,
"Hic!"

"These silver clothes will protect us from the erupting volcano," explained Mrs Zing. "But when you see all that fire and lava, you'll be so scared, you'll go, 'Eeek!' and your hiccups will disappear."

Suddenly, the volcano erupted.

"Eeek!" went Mrs Zing.

But Dreamboat Zing just lay on a rock and let the stream of lava carry him down the side of the volcano.

"It's just like a big firework," he
said. "And the silver clothes have
messed up my hair – that's all!
You see? Nothing scares me!"

So Mrs Zing took Dreamboat
Zing to a tropical island and
handed him a kite.

"What are you doing?" asked
Dreamboat Zing. Then added,
"Hic!"

"There'll be a hurricane soon,"
explained Mrs Zing. "When the
wind whisks you into the air and
you see tropical trees uprooted and
whirling around you, you'll be so
scared, you'll go, 'Eeek!' and your
hiccups will disappear."

Suddenly, a hurricane whisked
them into the air.

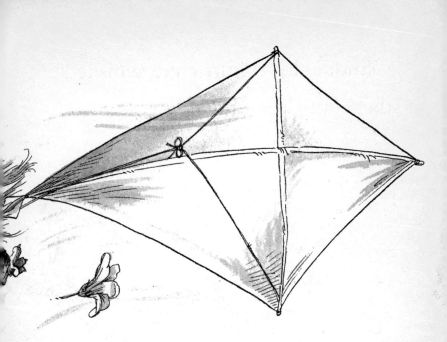

"Eeek!" went Mrs Zing.

But Dreamboat Zing just admired the view. "It's like a roller-coaster ride!" he said.

When he landed he was covered
in flowers. "These things have
brought on my hay fever and
made my eyes red – that's all!

"You see? Nothing scares me!
"Not a shark with a million
sharp teeth – Hic!

"Not a cave full of vampire bats – Hic!

"Not a volcano spurting fire
and lava – Hic!

"Not a hurricane uprooting
tropical trees – Hic!"

"You must be right," said Mrs
Zing. "Let's go home and have
dinner. I'm getting hungry."

When they got home,
Dreamboat Zing let out the
loudest "Eeek!" Mrs Zing had ever
heard.

"What's wrong?" she asked.

"An ugly monster!" Dreamboat
Zing replied.

"It's got red eyes!

"Messy hair!

"A dirty shirt!

"And a sharp tooth around its neck! It scared me!"

"But it's just you in the mirror," Mrs Zing told him. "Don't you remember?

"The flowers made your eyes red, the volcano messed up your hair, the bats got your shirt dirty and you made a necklace from the shark's tooth."

"Oh, cool," said Dreamboat Zing. Then added, "My hiccups have gone!"

"Thank goodness," replied Mrs
Zing.

"Shall I help you get dinner
ready?" asked Dreamboat Zing.

"Yes, please," replied Mrs Zing.
"All that travelling has tired me
out."

ready, steady, read!